OTHER BOOKS BY MARY SERFOZO AND KEIKO NARAHASHI:

Who Wants One?
Who Said Red?
(*Margaret K. McElderry Books*)

ALSO BY KEIKO NARAHASHI:
I Have a Friend
(*A Margaret K. McElderry Book*)

This book belongs to

_____

 An Early Start Edition from Macmillan Children's Book Clubs

RAIN TALK

RAIN TALK

Mary Serfozo
illustrated by Keiko Narahashi

Margaret K. McElderry Books

NEW YORK

To Maureen and Judith and sharing

M . S .

For Peter and Micah

K. N.

Margaret K. McElderry Books
Macmillan Publishing Company
866 Third Avenue
New York, New York 10022
Collier Macmillan Canada, Inc.

First Edition

10   9   8   7   6   5   4   3   2   1

Library of Congress Cataloging-in-Publication Data
Serfozo, Mary.
Rain talk/Mary Serfozo; illustrated by Keiko Narahashi.
—1st ed.   p   cm.
Summary: A child enjoys a glorious day in the rain, listening to
the varied sounds it makes as it comes down.
ISBN 0-689-50496-9
[1. Rain and rainfall—Fiction.]   I. Narahashi, Keiko, ill.
II. Title.   PZ7.S482Rai   1990   [E]—dc20
89-12178   CIP   AC

Ploomp go the first fat raindrops,

Ploomp Ploomp Ploomp
into the soft summer dust
of a country road.

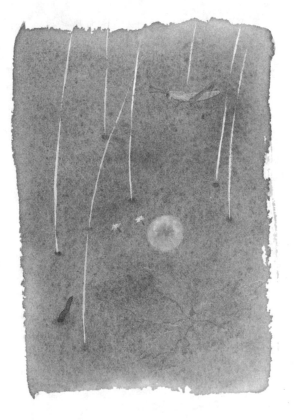

Each little drop digs a dark little hole
and the smell of wet dust tickles my nose.

On the old tin roof of the garden shed
the drops all try to talk at once...
Ping Ping PingaDing
Ping Ping Ping Ping Ping...

and they chuckle together
as they run down the drain.

It's raining harder now.
Listen to the
PlipPlipPlipPlipPlipPlip
as it speckles the smooth surface of the pond.

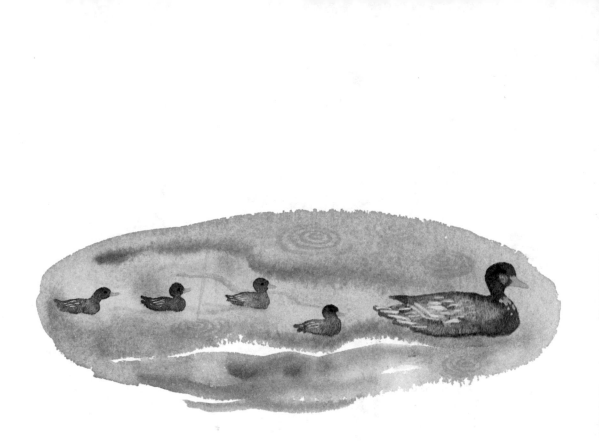

To Mother Duck
that says,
"Time to go for a swim."

Out on the highway
the raindrops bounce high,
and *Whoosh* and *Hiss*
as the cars hurry by.

Headlights are coming on,
reaching out to catch
the silvery slants of rain.

Now all I can hear
is the *Bup Bup Bup Bup*
of rain thumping on my umbrella...

and dropping and dripping all around.

Mother says to come in the house
and the rain tries to come in too...
*Flick...Flick...Flick*ing itself
like pebbles against the windowpanes.

I'd rather stay outside.

When I've had my supper and bath
I lie in front of the fire. And now and then
a raindrop slips down the chimney
to *Spit* and *Sizzle* on the logs.

I'm getting very sleepy here.

Tucked into my bed upstairs
I try to stay awake and listen to the
Drum-a-tum-a-Drum-a-tum-a-Drum-a-tum
on the roof above my head.

But my eyes...just won't...stay...open.

Tomorrow I may find the rain all gone,
with only a sparkle still caught
in a spiderweb or a flower.

But I'll look first...

for a rainbow!